M is for Mason Jar

A Homesteading Alphabet

by Carolyn
Bennett Fraiser

illustrations by
Sally Garland

Published by Familius LLC, www.familius.com
PO Box 1130, Sanger, CA 93657

Familius books are available at special discounts for bulk purchases,
whether for sales promotions or for family or corporate use. For more
information, contact Familius Sales at orders@familius.com.

Library of Congress Control Number: 2025933813

Print ISBN 9781641709668
Ebook ISBN 9798893960747

Printed in China

Edited by Leah Welker
Cover and book design by Brooke Jorden

10 9 8 7 6 5 4 3 2 1

First Edition

M is for Mason Jar

A Homesteading Alphabet

by Carolyn
Bennett Fraiser

illustrations by
Sally Garland

A is for attic
and armfuls of aprons our
aunties once made.

B is for baking
buttermilk biscuits for breakfast. Yum!

C is for canning
creamed corn and cucumbers from county fair cookbooks.

D is for dough
to make donuts with a dusting of sugar for dessert.

E is for eggs,
gathered extra early from excited hens.

F is for family

and faithful friends who farm and feast together.

G is for gardening

and growing a gallon of green beans with grandma.

H is for harvest
and a house full of honey and homegrown food.

I is for itching

from ivy and insects while investigating the fields.

J is for jellies
and prize-winning jams to be judged in June.

K is for kitchen,
where kindling is kept by the kettle for cocoa.

L is for livestock
and learning to labor and live off the land.

M is for mason jars

filled with marinades and marmalades with a hint of molasses.

N is for needles
to sew napkins and nightgowns and gifts for new neighbors.

O is for orchards
packed with oranges and olives on wide-open farms.

P is for pruning

the peach trees and pear trees with plenty of patience.

Q is for quilts

on queen-sized beds for quiet times and quick naps.

R is for root cellar

to store radishes and rosemary for all kinds of recipes.

S is for seeds
to scatter and sow in the soil next spring.

T is for tractors

that till up the dirt and make trails through the trees.

U is for untied boots
and long underwear, tucked unseen, under the bed.

V is for visitors,
who buy vegetables and vanilla beans plucked off the vine.

W is for windmills
that pump water from wells all winter long.

X is for X-ing—
chicken X-ing, duck X-ing, and goat X-ing.

Y is for yule logs
and year-end traditions with both young and old.

Z is for zippers
on cozy sleeping bags and dozing under the stars.
Good night. Sleep tight. Zzzzz . . .

26 Ways Kids Can Get Involved on a Homestead

- Find an apron that fits just right.
- Measure the ingredients for batter.
- Gather the spices and supplies for canning.
- Roll and cut the dough for biscuits or donuts.
- Collect eggs from the henhouse.
- Help your family prep the soil for planting.
- Pick vegetables from the garden.
- Make gifts for friends and neighbors.
- Remember to use insect repellant before going outside.
- Enter your favorite items in county fair competitions.
- Help the grownups cook dinner.
- Volunteer to feed the animals.
- Collect, wash, and sort mason jars.
- Measure fabric for sewing projects.
- Pick fruit from trees.
- Carry a basket of supplies to the garden.
- Help fold quilts and blankets after taking a nap.
- Prepare potatoes, radishes, and garlic for storage.
- Learn how and why to seed-save for next year.
- Take a ride on the tractor with a grownup.
- Clean up under the beds.
- Greet people who visit your homestead.
- Pump and fill water buckets and troughs on the farm.
- Make sure pens for all the animals are always latched.
- Help carry the wood for the fireplace or wood stove.
- Spend a night outdoors under the stars.